unbroken

YOUR LOSS WILL BE HIS GAIN.

SUTTON SNOW

UNBROKEN

SUTTON SNOW

CONTENTS

Content Warning	1
Theme Song	3
Untitled	5
Prologue	11
Prologue	21
Chapter 1	33
Chapter 2	41
Chapter 3	55
Chapter 4	63
Chapter 5	73
Chapter 6	79
Chapter 7	89
Chapter 8	99
Chapter 9	111
Chapter 10	123
Chapter 11	133
Chapter 12	143
Chapter 13	151
Chapter 14	163
Chapter 15	171
Chapter 16	177
Epilogue	187
Pacey's Story	193
Acknowledgments	195
About Sutton Snow	199
About Tinley Blake	203
Author Works	207

content warning

Theme
song

Dirty Harry by SAY GRACE

dedication

For every woman who has ever been betrayed.
You are a rockstar.
A queen.
Dust yourself off and make him pay.

seven
months
earlier

weston

prologue

"THANKS FOR COMING, man. I really think you're gonna like these guys." Asher kicks out a bar chair and gestures for me to sit.

"Not a problem. I'm pretty full right now, but I'm always willing to listen." Ignoring the seat, I grab a handful of peanuts from the bowl on the table. Cracking one, I chuck the shells on the floor into the sea of others lying there and nod hello to Pacey.

"They should be up next."

"Perfect. I'm gonna grab a beer. Anyone need anything?"

"Nah, Carson went to piss and then he's grabbing us a round," Pacey says, eyeing a hot blonde across the room.

Sidestepping multiple people, I eventually make my way across the room. The place is packed for noon on a Thursday.

I lean against the end of the bar and wait for the bartender to finish up with a woman halfway down. My eyes trail down her body, lingering on the curve of her ass for a second. Her fingers tap on the wooden surface in beat with the band playing. Her hair is piled high on her head in a bun with whisps of brunette curls escaping to tickle her face.

It's been almost two years since Maggie and I split up. With the exception of one or two quick fucks, no one has grabbed my attention . . . until now. I've poured myself into work, producing many new and up and coming artists. Just last week, one of them made it to number one on the Billboard charts.

The man behind the bar fills a glass with ice and Coke before passing it to her along with an envelope filled with cash. *Probably her paycheck,* I think to myself. She sits on a stool and sips the Coke.

I order a beer and pass the bartender a five-dollar bill. Tilting the bottle back, I take a swig and watch the woman. Her eyes are closed now, like she's absorbing the music playing on stage, but something about the way she holds herself calls to me. Her shoulders are tense, her body on edge, even though I can sense she's attempting to let it all go. It reminds me a bit of a bird getting ready to take flight.

"Shit, who drug you out of the studio?" Carson says, sliding onto a stool next to where I'm standing. His strawberry blond hair is longer than the last time I saw him, almost as long as it was when we were kids, stirring up trouble in the neighborhood.

"Fucking Ash. He found a band that he wants me to hear."

"Thought you were full?"

"I am." I grunt. "But you know how he is."

"Yeah. Stubborn as fuck when he wants something."

My gaze travels back down the bar, but the woman is gone. Heaving a sigh of disappointment, I grab my beer off the counter and walk away, leaving Carson alone.

After a quick check of the stage to make sure the band isn't swapping out yet, I make a detour for the restroom. As I round the corner, something collides with my chest. I stumble back a step before looking down. Swollen, red-rimmed, hazel eyes meet mine.

"I'm so sorry. I didn't see you."

My hand wraps around her elbow, steadying her. She swipes her fingers across her face, drying the tears from her face.

"It's fine, Little Dove. No harm, no foul. Are you okay?"

"Truthfully? No. My life feels like it's spiraling out of control, and I can't even take a single moment to try to stop the epic tailspin because I'm too busy wandering this God-forsaken city looking for my mother, who's probably about two sheets to the wind and half naked with today's flavor of the week."

"Take a deep breath. It's going to be okay."

"Okay? How's it going to be okay? My life hasn't been okay for at least a decade." She's rambling, working herself up more and more with each passing second. It would be cute if it weren't clear that she's emotionally hurting right now.

" . . . and on top of all that, if I don't find her before I go home, I'll get to spend the rest of my birthday alone with the scumbag boyfriend she let move in."

Her face is flushed, and tears pool in her eyes, once again threatening to fall. I've never liked to see a woman cry. It's my kryptonite, so before those tears can fall, I do the only thing I can think of to take her mind off all that. I press my lips to hers.

She gasps against my mouth, and I take the opening to slide my tongue into her mouth and tangle with her own. Her arms fall slack. I wrap my own arm around her waist and pull her body roughly against mine. The music and crowd fade away, lost in the background. Nothing else matters but her mouth on mine.

After a few minutes, I slow the kiss. I feel her body tense when the last few minutes registers. She takes a step back, her eyes wide. Her fingers trace the plump line of her lip. "You . . . you kissed me."

"I did."

"You had no right."

"I didn't hear you complaining."

She raises an arm, fully intending to slap me. I can see the thought play out across her face. I wrap my hand around hers and step close to her, leaning down to whisper in her ear.

"It was just a kiss, but you follow through with that thought and I won't be able to stop what comes next."

Her arm drops back to her side before she pushes past me. I stand there watching her as she storms across the bar and out the exit.

lucy

epilogue

I CHECK four more bars before finding my mother. As expected, she's half naked in a back corner with a man who smells like he hasn't bathed in weeks. Grabbing her arm, I pull her toward the exit, blocking out the screeching words coming from her mouth.

This is getting so fucking old.

But the alternative is even worse. I know. I let her run off a few months ago and didn't bother tracking her down. By the time she showed back up, her entire monthly check had been blown on booze and drugs. The following week, our power was shut off, and three days after that, the water too. I was forced to take every available shift at the diner to scrape together enough to get them turned back on.

It's my eighteenth birthday. I should be on top of the world, yet I've spent all day searching for her.

I don't release my grip on her arm until we are walking up the steps at home. She's sullen and thankfully quiet for once. "She's your problem now. Try not to let her run off again . . . or do. I don't really care." For once, my mom's boyfriend keeps his mouth shut.

I already dug the other half of her cash out of the front pocket of her jeans and shoved it in my purse. Monday morning, I'll deposit it in my account and pay the bills, but right now I need to shower and try to wash the feel of that man's lips from my memory.

Who the hell kisses a complete stranger? I mean, I suppose he was probably trying to get me to stop word vomiting my life's problems at his feet, but still. It's inappropriate. And just wrong. Even if it felt surprisingly perfect. In that moment, I hadn't thought of anything. Not my mother, not the bills or school, or even the fact that I'd spent my entire birthday traipsing across town, from bar to bar.

Luckily, I have built up a rapport with a lot of the bartenders. They turn their heads when I come looking, even though up until today, I was underage and technically still too young to drink. Joe always cashes my mom's check for her every month and puts the money aside for me to pick up later. Without him, I don't know what I would do.

My phone dings with a text. Glancing down, I see Malcom's name appear.

Jesus. Malcom. No way was I telling him what happened. I didn't ask for it. It just happened.

So what if I liked it. It doesn't matter.

I shoot off a reply, letting him know I'll be ready by six thirty, and then I step into a steaming shower.

Exactly twenty-nine minutes later, I'm walking out the door and climbing in the front passenger seat of his Jeep. Malcom leans over and presses a kiss to my lips in greeting. I force myself to not compare his with the man in the bar.

"How was your day?" he asks, shifting into drive.

"It was good. And yours?"

We spend the next ten minutes with him telling me about football practice and some new guy on the team. I zone out for most of the conversation until we turn onto a paved drive and pass through an open gate. Holy shit. I knew Malcom's family was well off, but I didn't expect this.

His house is huge. At least three stories, white plaster exterior. It's simple, but beautiful with multileveled balconies that connect each floor and lead around the side of the house on the lowest level.

When Malcom first invited me to this, I'd turned him down. It seemed a strange way to meet his dad for the first time, surrounded by a group of other people I didn't know and had no idea how to fit in with, but eventually, he wore me down.

Cars line the circular drive. I watch as a few people make their way inside, each one dressed better than the last. My skinny jeans and shirt pale in comparison, but before I can back out and request that he take home, he's opening my door and helping me down. His hand slides in mine, and the smile spreading across his face is bright enough to stop the heart of any woman.

Except my own. Which doesn't so much as leap.

I can do this. It's just a small get together. I mentally encourage myself with each step toward the front door. Then we're inside. My chest tightens when everyone turns to glance our way. I squeeze Malcom's hand, and he gives a gentle brush of his thumb across the back of my hand before pulling me through the crowd.

"Dad. I've got someone I want you to meet."

The small crowd parts, and I watch the floor, focused on putting one foot in front of the other. When we stop, I raise my gaze and lock eyes with last person I ever expected to see again.

A giggle escapes. Then another. I push my hand against my mouth, trying to stop the insanity bubbling out of my chest. Only me. Only my life could be this damn bizarre. I swear, at some point, I must have pissed off God because across from me, humor dancing in his dark brown eyes, is the man from the bar.

"Hi. I'm Weston, Malcom's dad. I don't think I caught your name."

Malcom is watching me, worry creasing his eyes. But I can't be bothered with what he thinks right now. "Lucy," I say, taking his hand. My skin pebbles the moment our flesh connects. Goosebumps break out across my arms.

"Lucy. It's nice to formally meet you."

Someone pulls Malcom away, leaving me alone in the middle of the room with his dad. Weston runs a finger across my pebbled skin before leaning in and whispering in my ear, "If you wanted to see me again, all you had to do was ask."

Holy fuck buckets.

I kissed Malcom's dad. And to make matters worse, I really want to do it again.

present
day

weston

chapter one

LUCY THRUSTS the back door open and slams it behind her. Her face is flushed, her eyes wild as she scans the kitchen. When she sees me standing there, she takes a deep breath and tries to calm her breathing.

"Are you okay?"

"I'm fine."

Her curls cling to her skin. She pushes them away with a swipe of her hand and leans against the counter. I might be pushing forty, but some things are ageless. When a woman says she's fine, it's a lie. I grab a bottle of water from the fridge and step close to her. She tenses, barely, but I notice and stop before reaching her to hold out the bottle. She takes it from me and relaxes a fraction before twisting the cap and taking a long sip of the water. When she finishes, her hazel-green eyes meet mine.

I lean against the island opposite her and let my gaze travel the length of her body. She's not short, standing at about five-six, but she's so tiny she seems smaller. The shorts she's wearing hug her frame in all the right spots, and I physically force myself to stop looking at her. She isn't mine, and even if she weren't dating my son, she's still too young for me.

A fact I'm forced to remember every time I see her.

"I bet you're glad to finally be done with school."

She huffs a little. "I guess. Mostly, I'm just ready to be out of the house. If I have to live there one more second, I think I might scream."

I knew Lucy had issues at home, but she's never been very talkative about them, and it wasn't ever my place to push. When I first met her, before I knew she was dating Malcom, she was in a bar, hunting for her mother. "Is it that bad?" I ask.

"It's fucking hell."

"What do you have planned?"

"I don't know. I've been saving so I can get a place of my own. Becca and I were thinking about splitting something, but then she got accepted to the university." She stares off in her own mind for a moment then shakes her head. "I'm sorry. I didn't mean to unload all of that on you." She takes a breath, squaring her shoulders. "The graduation party sounds like it's a hit."

I weigh my next words carefully, wanting her to know she can talk to me but also not wanting to scare her off. "You know you're more than welcome to stay here."

She laughs humorlessly. "I'm not sure that would work out well."

"Why do you say that?"

She turns to face me, her body less than a foot away now, and meets my gaze before replying, "You don't think that would be strange?" She tilts her head to the side and rakes her eyes up my body. "Me staying here without Malcom. Alone . . . with you."

I don't know what to say. Yes? No? Fuck. When I first met Lucy seven months ago, it was under very different circumstances, and then she popped up on Malcom's arm and my world shifted on its axis.

"You love Malcom and he loves you. I don't know why he would have a problem with you here."

She scoffs, almost like she's irritated with my response. I don't know what to think about that. "Right. I'm sure you're right. Where is he, by the way?"

"Last I saw him, he was in the den with a couple of guys from the football team." She grabs the bottle of water from the counter and moves to step past me. I wrap my hand around her wrist, pulling her to a stop. She stumbles into my chest. "If there's something you aren't saying, I can't help, Little Dove."

Her breath hitches in her chest. Her eyes focus on my lips as they move, and her tongue darts out, moistening her own. Her body leans into mine, and I inhale her intoxicating scent. Every instinct in me is screaming to pull her close and press my mouth to hers. I haven't once forgotten the feel of her lips on mine, the taste of her tongue as it danced in my mouth.

"I'm f—"

"Don't tell me you're fine. Don't do that. It's obvious you're shaken up. If you don't want to talk about it, I'll let it go. But don't ever feel like you have to hide behind placating words. It's okay to not be okay."

"I just . . . I can't."

"I understand. But my offer still stands. Just say the word, and I'll have a room ready for you."

"Thanks. I appreciate the offer."

"Anytime, Little Dove."

This time when she brushes past me, I don't stop her.

lucy

chapter Two

THE HOUSE IS overrun with our graduating class. Everywhere I look, red Solo cups are being passed around and tossed back with vigor. The idea of getting drunk doesn't sound appealing, so I keep a tight grip on my bottle of water and go hunt for Malcom.

I find him on the back deck a few minutes later, puncturing a beer can with a key and chugging the contents while a group of people chant him on. "Drink. Drink. Drink."

He tosses the empty can in a growing pile in the grass and pulls me to him. His breath smells like trash, a mixture of cheap booze and stale cigarettes. I hold my breath when he pushes his sloppy, wet lips to mine. "Hey, baby. Wanna give it a try?"

I slip an arm around his waist and turn my head away from his seeking mouth. "Looks like you're having fun."

"I'm reigning champ so far, but who knows? Maybe you'll take my crown the same way you took my heart." His words are slurred and barely understandable.

"I'm good," I say, releasing him and stepping away. He doesn't notice. Instead, he raises his hands in the air, cheering on the next round of competitors.

The truth is that I never intended to make Malcom fall for me. I'm still not a hundred percent sure this thing between us can even be classified as love. Infatuation, maybe. For the most part, I think Malcom sees me as a game to win. We've been seeing each other for almost seven months now, and the farthest he has gotten is second base. Not because I don't want to have sex. On the contrary, the idea excites me. But every time I close my eyes and picture a man touching me that way, it's Weston I see.

It doesn't take a rocket scientist to see why that's a problem. Even if he wasn't Malcom's father, he's still twenty-something years my senior and not even a little interested.

Maybe once . . . before he knew.

It doesn't help that he's so damn kind and caring, always going out of his way to check on me and make sure I'm okay. Every single time he's within three feet of me, I imagine leaping into his arms, the memories of our kiss consuming me . . . the feel of his scruffy beard against my cheek, those full lips locked with mine.

"Phew, girl, you are flushed. How many have you had tonight?" Becca waves her hand in my face.

"Enough," I say, not bothering to mention that I haven't drunk a single sip. The flush on my face has nothing to do with alcohol.

"Better stick to water for now. Looks like Malcom is about done too. Guess you won't be losing your V-card tonight. He's going to have whisky dick." I love Becca, really. But sometimes, my best friend has a habit of saying whatever pops in her head. Most days, it's fine. But sometimes, I'd like to not know her every thought.

I sigh and turn around. Sure enough, he's chugging another beer and swaying on his feet. He takes a step to steady himself and overcorrects. One second, he's balancing on the edge of the deck and the next, he's tumbling headfirst into the pool.

The rest of the guys standing around take that

as a cue to jump in with him, none of them bothering to notice it wasn't intentional.

I glance at wide-eyed Becca. "Jesus. Help me drag him out, will you?"

Setting my bottle of water on a vacant chair, I lean over the edge of the pool. He's in the shallow end but doesn't seem to register that fact. His feet are kicking in the water, trying to keep his head above the water's edge. I toss my shirt on the deck and slip the shorts down, then ease my way into the cool water. Once I reach him, I slip an arm under his and half drag, half pull him to the stairs. It takes a few minutes to get him out of the water, even with Becca taking his other side, but we manage to get him propped up on a lounge chair.

Becca grabs a couple of towels and passes them to me. I wrap one around my torso, covering my two-piece, and lay the other over him to soak up as much of the water as possible before pulling him back to his feet. "Come on, let's get you inside."

The house seems less packed now than it did an hour ago. I coax Malcom down the hall, thankful that his bedroom isn't on the second floor. I don't know how I would've gotten him up the steps tonight. He's barely coherent now.

He makes a beeline for the bed, but I force him to wait while I peel his shirt and shorts off. He really is an incredibly attractive guy. In a few more years, he might look more like his father.

An image of Weston pops in my head, no shirt, with slick swim trunks stuck to his thighs.

God, get it together, Lucy.

Malcom falls sideways onto the bed, pulling me with him. We land in a heap on top of his gray comforter, and then his arms and hands are traveling across my flesh. Every time I get one hand moved, another is there. "Come on, baby, what's one day? I want you."

"No, Malcom. Not yet." He knows I won't budge. And besides, it's only one more day until we go on the trip. He's waited this long. He can damn sure wait until he's able to stay awake for it.

Malcom pulls his hands away and tosses them over his face, pretending to pout. A few minutes later, soft snores fill the room. I ease from the bed, taking Malcom's wet clothes from the floor, and gently close the bedroom door behind me.

I don't know how much time has passed, but when I step out of the room, the party seems to be winding down. The music is still playing, but at a much more discreet volume. I step into the laundry room and toss Malcom's clothes into the washer along with both of our towels. My swimsuit has almost completely dried, so I grab a tee shirt from a basket on the dryer and slip it over my head. When I exit, I walk straight into Weston.

"Oof." Breath is forced out of me when I collide with him.

"Sorry. I didn't see you there. Malcom?"

"He's in bed, sound asleep," I say, leaning against the doorframe.

"And you?" he asks, tilting his head questioningly.

I swallow, trying to settle my nerves. It seems like every time I turn around, I'm running into the man. "Just putting some wet clothes in the wash and about to start cleaning up."

"You don't have to do that. I've got it."

I nod, watching his mouth as he speaks. "I know, but I can't sleep right now. My mind won't shut off so it will help."

"Okay." He passes me a large black garbage bag. "I already got the kitchen. We can tackle out back together."

We fill garbage bags with discarded beer cans in silence. I wasn't lying when I said my mind wouldn't shut off. For weeks now, I've been contemplating what to do about Malcom. It's not that I don't like him, I do. But it feels like we have very different outlooks on life and where we want to see ourselves. He's fine partying and living his best life. After earlier today, moving out of my mother's house is now at the top of my priority list, which means no partying and lots of hard work.

And if I'm being honest with myself, my attraction to Malcom is almost nonexistent. He's still the best option for losing my V card. My only other option is to toss it away to some stranger or a guy I barely know. At least with Malcom, I know he'll be gentle. But is that all I get? Just someone who is kind and gentle? What about passion? Shouldn't I wait until I find a man who makes my blood sing and my pulse race? Someone who erases all my fear with his touch?

I toss my full bag in a pile next to Weston's and gaze across the yard. A moment later, Weston joins me at the edge of the pool.

"You want to talk about it?" he asks.

I turn toward him, running my gaze across his body. The man is mysterious and intimidating as hell. It always feels as if his dark eyes are peering straight into my soul. And he's so . . . intelligent and well-spoken, his voice like soft butter on a warm piece of toast. Don't even get me started on how utterly handsome he is. Tall and toned, with thick jet-black hair, the same color as the well-manicured beard on his chiseled jaw.

"No, not really. What I want is to forget it all for a minute and just let loose. For once, I want to feel free."

He nods his head, taking in what I've said. "I take it cleaning didn't help empty your mind."

I chuckle dryly. "Not even a little."

"Want to take a swim? That usually helps me."

Shrugging my shoulders, I eye the water. A swim does sound nice. The water was perfect earlier, but I really need to get to bed. We have an early day tomorrow.

"Just stop thinking for a minute and leap."

I laugh. "Is that philosophical?"

Weston takes a step toward me, a wicked gleam in his eye. "Hey, don't knock it until you try it."

"You first, then."

I've no sooner finished the sentence than he dives into the pool, spraying water into the air.

"Jesus."

"I told you. Don't think, just leap."

Taking a deep breath, I shut out all thoughts, and for the first time in my life, I simply jump. The water is cool and refreshing. Spreading my arms, I glide underwater using my feet to propel me faster. I dart past Weston and then circle back around him. His arms dip under the water, trying to catch me, but his fingers brushing across my breast and sparks race across my skin.

When my lungs feel like they will pop without oxygen, I surface, taking in several short gasps of air. A strong hand wraps around the back of my neck, his fingers encircling my throat. His grip is not gentle, but it's not forceful either. He's holding me in place. When he leans forward, his body presses against my back. "Caught you." Chills spread across every inch of my flesh.

I spin around to face him, but he sinks beneath the water and swims past my legs, only to pop up behind me once again.

My pulse is racing, thrumming in my ears like the beat of a drum. Every place he touches me tingles. I dive forward, propelling away from him. There's a splash, but I don't waste a second looking back. I've almost reached the far wall when his hand wraps around my ankle and pulls me back toward him. His arm circles my waist, followed by a short snip of teeth against my shoulder.

Pushing against the bottom of the pool, I dart to the surface and spin, looking for him, waiting for him to surface. A few seconds later, he pops up by the steps in the shallow end. He shakes the water out of his hair and slowly climbs from the pool.

"Do you always go around biting people?" I say, rubbing my fingers across the indent of his teeth.

"Only those who run."

He steps fully from the pool and turns away from me to grab a towel, but not before I see the massive erection tenting his shorts. My retort dies on my tongue, shrivels to ash, and blows away on the wind.

"Come on, let's get you to bed. We have to be up early tomorrow."

"I'm fully capable of getting myself to bed, thank you very much."

But I climb from the pool anyway and lift a hand to take the spare towel from him. Instead of passing it to me like a normal person, he wraps it around my chest tightly, his fingers brushing innocently along my flesh before tucking it into itself between my breasts.

My mind empties of all thought, replaced by a growing need to feel his hands everywhere. I lift my head to meet his darkened gaze. I could do it. I could step forward and press my lips to his. My gaze darts to the patio door. Everyone is either gone or asleep. If I wanted to do this, no one would know.

I pull my eyes back to his and decide that for

once, I will throw all caution to the wind. I will do what I want, and damn the consequences. But he steps back, and the moment is gone, lost in the abyss. "Next time, Little Dove."

"Next time?" I ask, confusion lacing my tone.

"Just leap."

weston

chapter three

I WAKE before the rest of the house and make a pot of coffee. Once the sweet aroma is filling the house, I walk to both Malcom and Elisa's doors and knock until I hear them moving around.

Lucy is the first to stick her head out, then Elisa. I hold up my coffee mug and point toward the kitchen. "Fifteen minutes, then were loading up."

Fuck.

I thought I'd gotten myself under control after last night, but the only thing better than Lucy in a bikini is fresh-faced, just crawled from the bed Lucy. I want to wrap my hands in her hair and bury my face in her neck.

I could see the thoughts play out across her

face last night. It would've been so easy to stand there and wait for her make a move, but I didn't want her to think about wanting me or to play out the consequences and repercussions in her head. I want her to want me so badly she doesn't think at all, only instinct driving her actions.

Fifteen minutes later, we're loading up the back of the Bronco and getting ready to hit the road. The rest of the guys are already on the road. Pacey called to let me know they were leaving about ten minutes ago.

Every year since we graduated college, we've taken this trip. Sometimes to a different site, but always together. Once I married and had Malcom, he started coming along too. It's the one thing we all manage to agree on, even now. We don't miss this trip. It's a chance to reconnect and catch up.

This is the first year Elisa has joined us. When Malcom asked if his stepsister could come along, I almost said no. I didn't want to speak to Maggie to clear it with her. The last conversation with my ex-wife hadn't exactly been pleasant.

But then I thought of Lucy being there with a bunch of men and figured she might welcome the company.

Malcom opens the passenger door and gestures for Lucy to climb in. "You can ride up front."

"Are you sure? Elisa can sit up here, and we can ride in the back together."

"I'm good. You can have the front. I'd hate for you to barf in the back," Elisa says, climbing into the back seat.

"Everyone in."

My command seems to jolt Lucy into action. She crawls in the front seat and pulls the door closed before latching the seat belt and staring out the windshield. Her shoulders are tense, and she takes small breaths like she's on the verge of crying.

"Guess that means you get aux, Little Dove."

Her lip lifts slightly as she takes the phone from my hand. "Just one rule. You have to mix it up."

Her eyes light up with the challenge.

Fifteen minutes into the drive, I'm starting to think having her up front was a horrible idea. My hand itches to reach across and run along her thigh or tuck the hair behind her ear. Malcom is passed out in the back seat, Elisa leaning on his shoulder asleep as well.

The song changes, and Lucy bounces in her seat when it starts. "Oh my God, I love this song. Seriously. It's one of my top three favorites." She reaches over and turns up the volume, her eyes lighting up with an internal flame.

When the first line starts, she closes her eyes, swaying in the seat, and sings, *She never mentions the word "addiction".*

Fucking hell.

My dick hardens instantly, the urge to pull this truck over and bury myself inside her almost more than I can fight.

lucy

chapter four

THREE HOURS into the trip and I'm already regretting my decision to come. It's not that I don't like camping. I love the woods and nature, the calming stillness of it all.

We turn off the main road onto a smaller, less traveled dirt road. Dust billows behind the Bronco. I watch it in the side mirror until we finally roll to a stop. Malcom climbs out the back, Elisa right behind him. When my feet hit the solid ground, I stretch and try to work out my tense muscles from the long drive.

Three hours of nothing but music playing on the stereo. It wouldn't have been uncomfortable, but after last night, with the way Weston and I . . . It wasn't like I could talk about it. Not with

Malcom in the backseat, even if he was asleep most of the ride.

I went to Malcom's room after the dip in the pool, and once I was alone again, all those pesky thoughts came racing back. I stood at the foot of the bed and watched Malcom sleep for a minute, and not once did I think about waking him. Ten minutes earlier, I was ready to jump his dad's bones, but there with him . . . nothing.

The smart move would be to end it now.

"I'll be right back. I want to show Elisa something I found last year." Malcom takes off before I can open my mouth. It shouldn't irritate me, but it does. Why couldn't he show me too?

Reaching back into the Bronco, I grab my water bottle and phone. Weston pops the back of the truck open and starts pulling stuff out. I take a quick sip of water and check my messages, then toss them both back in the seat before peeking my head around the side.

"Need some help?"

"Sure. Grab that tent there." He nods in the direction of a grey plastic covered bag.

I reach in and pull it free.

"We'll set up and then unpack the rest so we have somewhere to put everything."

"Makes sense."

Another truck pulls in behind us, sliding across the gravel before coming to a full stop. A moment later, the driver is walking over. He's easily six two, with curly blond hair and bright blue eyes. His shirt is stretched across his arms, and I eye it for a second, wondering if he's really that buff or if he bought a smaller size to seem that way.

"Wes, please tell me you have an extra tent in there."

"Forgot the most important thing, Carson?"

"Well, fuck no. It flew off the back on the highway. I thought I saw something but wasn't sure until I got here."

"I only brought two," Weston says.

"What sizes?" he asks.

"Ten- to twelve-person, and a four- to six."

"You think your bunch can squeeze in the bigger one for the weekend?" He turns, pleading. I almost snicker.

Weston glances over at me, and Carson follows his look.

"Yeah, we can manage. Lucy, toss that to him."

I step forward, holding the tent out in front of me. "Lucy? I'm Carson. It's nice to meet you. You wanna help me set this up?"

Weston growls in his direction. Literally growls out a warning. Carson steps back, holding his hands in the air. "Damn. Off limits. Got it." Then he turns to me and whispers conspiratorially, "If you get tired of the broody one, you know where to find me."

"I'm not . . . we're not. It's not . . ."

"Lucy is Malcom's girlfriend."

"Oh, yeah? Good for him. Where is the little squirt, anyway?"

I don't stay to hear the rest of the conversation. Grabbing the other tent from the back, I walk to the place marked for setup and start pulling the pieces out of the bag and laying them in a row. When all the poles are inserted and it's ready to be staked down, Weston appears. "Let's point the door toward the lake."

I grab the tent and start shifting it around. "Carson can be a little extreme. Just ignore him."

"Oh, he didn't bother me."

"Good."

We finish setting up and then unload the rest of the supplies. An hour later, Malcom still isn't back, and I'm beyond irritated now. "I'm going to put this stuff down by the pier."

I nod, lost in thought. And then I'm alone.

Utterly alone.

The silence is starting to become more of an enemy than a friend.

To be fair, I'm partially responsible for my gloomy mood. I built up this wonderful idea in my head, created so many romantic ideas of what this weekend would entail. Even if Malcom isn't the man I really wanted to spend it with. It was better than the backseat of a car or behind the bleachers at a football game like Becca.

I even went as far as imagining how that moment would go. Hell, I've been imagining that moment the way some girls picture their weddings.

You know . . . *the* moment.

This is the weekend I planned to give up my V-card. I even started birth control a couple of months ago so there wouldn't be any *surprises* later.

My mother didn't want me to end up like her, pregnant at sixteen without the means to take care of a baby. As soon as I was old enough to understand about the birds and the bees, she sat me down and made me promise to wait until I finished high school to have sex. That promise has now been fulfilled.

Not that it was hard or anything. Malcom was my first real boyfriend. Before him, I never really had any interest in dating. Something else my mom bestowed in me—a strong distrust in men.

Actually, I think my dad had a hand in that one too.

He left before I was born. Met the bastard once, when I was around eleven. He was between stints in jail, pretending he was going to do better. Be better. That lasted all of two weeks.

He robbed some old lady the day after we met and was quickly shipped back off to prison.

Good riddance.

Malcom has always been unique, though— kind and caring. At least he used to be. Lately, he's been different. Hell, maybe that's my fault too. I've been so on the fence about us that he could have sensed something was wrong.

That's why I originally wanted to come on this trip, why I was so sure he was the right person to take that step with even if there was no passion, no overbearing desire to be with him. But so far, this weekend is nothing like I was expecting. I damn sure didn't anticipate being abandoned the moment we pulled into the campsite and unloaded. I mean, who would? And yet, that's exactly what Malcom did.

Fed up with sitting here by myself, I peer around the campsite and listen for Malcom. Birds chirp overhead, the trees rustle in the breeze, but there's still no sign of my boyfriend.

Fuck this.

I duck back into the tent and swap my worn Birkenstocks for Doc Martens, rubbing some homemade tea tree oil bug repellant on. When Malcom still hasn't returned after another five minutes, I take off through the woods in the direction he headed earlier.

weston

chapter five

WHEN I FINISH SETTING up the fishing gear, Asher and Pacey are pulling up and Lucy is nowhere to be seen. I spend a few minutes with the guys, every second grating. Not just at the thought of Lucy alone in the woods. The girl has been camping before. She knows what to do and how to take care of herself.

But she ran off.

And every second I stand around talking, she's getting farther and farther away.

The idea of hunting her down has my pulse racing and my dick hardening.

I warned her. I like the chase, and more than that, I live for the capture.

My Little Dove doesn't know what she has started, but she will. Oh, she will.

And this time when I catch her, *she's mine.*

I don't bother telling anyone I'm leaving. They are all grown and can handle themselves. I have a woman to track down.

Stepping off the path, I tilt my head and listen for the sound of her footfalls. They are distant, but I can hear them. Taking off in that direction, I spot her up ahead. When I reach that spot, however, I stop. Directly across from where I'm standing, I just barely make out the outline of her body. But what I see makes my mouth run dry. She's touching herself, running a hand between her thighs and up. Her skirt lifts, but I can't see much else.

I take a step closer, needing to be near her. The desire to watch her bring herself pleasure is intense.

Or even better, to taste her. To feel her soft skin against mine. I need her like a fire needs oxygen.

lucy

chapter six

SOFT MOANS PULL me off the path, curiosity luring me toward the sound, toward the couple hidden among the trees. The crunching of leaves under my feet causes my footsteps to slow as I inch closer. There's a woman lying on a huge rock, her head thrown back and legs spread wide, her full breasts rising and falling. A man's head moves between her thighs. The sound of suckling echoes around me.

Her hand twines in his hair, her moans growing louder, more urgent. My stomach flutters in response, and warmth spreads across my body. My nipples pebble and my own breasts feel heavier under my crop top. Moisture pools between my thighs, and my hand wanders there before I even realize what's happening. I run my fingers across my thigh, under the flowy skirt, over my panties, my eyes focused on the man's head between her thighs. He slowly licks up her slit then back down, over and over again, before focusing on the bud at the top. My fingers find my own bundles of nerves, my legs starting to twitch, warmth spreading from my stomach through my entire body.

No one else has ever touched me here, let alone kissed, licked, or sucked my sensitive flesh. But I'm suddenly desperate for it.

There's something so very enticing and erotic about secretly watching them—watching the sensual dance of nature's most natural act. The act of coming together, two bodies primed and flush, becoming one.

My cheeks heat when I imagine a man between my legs, doing these things to my body. It's like the world opened, offering me a sign. This weekend is perfect. You've waited long enough. Take what you want.

I slide a finger under the seam of my panties and run it through the wetness there. My breath hitches in my throat. So close. I am so close to losing myself right here, right now. It's not the first time I've touched myself, but this feels different, better, my orgasm building quickly. Biting my lip, I dip a finger inside my wet pussy, pretending Weston is between my legs licking and savoring every drip of my pussy, my fingers pumping in and out of me.

Goosebumps form on my skin, an eerie feeling washing over me. I freeze up with fear, my gaze darting across the forest.

Weston.

His intense stare is locked on me, his chest quickly rising and falling. He'd been watching me touch myself. The thought should horrify me, but my blood only grows hotter.

He takes a step toward me, his foot cracking a branch underneath, breaking my trance. Time stands still as I glance back at the couple and the man lifts his head. The birds quit chirping. My heart no longer beats in my chest. My lungs are unable to pump air.

It's no stranger at all. The man is Malcom. And the girl . . . Elisa.

I stare in horror, unable to move. I don't know what's more shocking, the fact that he's cheating on me, or the fact that he's . . .

Elisa grabs his face and pulls him in for a kiss, her hands fumbling with his jeans. She frees his cock and guides it to her entrance.

Seeing him thrust into her finally releases me

from whatever was keeping me immobile, and I run.

Branches cut into my skin, thorny bushes threatening to trip and impale me with each stumbling stretch of my legs. It doesn't matter, I'm desperate to get away as quickly as possible. If I can just get back to the campsite . . .

No. *Home.*

I need to go home.

How could I be so stupid? So blind? I honestly planned to have sex with him this weekend, fully intended to give him the most sacred piece of myself. The thoughts crash through my mind like waves against a rocky shore, each one barreling into me harder and faster than the last. I slow and gulp down mouthfuls of air, trying to build a damn against the thoughts, rock after rock stacked against the overwhelming waves.

Fuck Malcom.

Oops, looks like someone beat you to that.

Prick.

Yes. He indeed knows how to use his prick.

My chest feels tight, tears streaming down my face. I swipe my hand across my face, drying the moisture. Malcom isn't worth it. And I'm not sad.

I'm fucking furious.

The crunch of branches behind me tells me

I've got company. It may be the cowardly thing to do, but I don't give him the chance to catch up, the burning inferno of rage propelling me even faster. I don't want to hear a single word out of Malcom's mouth.

By the time my feet stop moving, I have no clue where I am. At some point, I took a left instead of going right and back toward the campsite. A creeping dread washes over me when I realize my phone is back in the tent. I'm lost with no way to call for help.

Clouds are moving in, the sun that was shining bright and warm now muted, the gray sky peeking through the canopy of the trees. It will be dark soon.

My anger quickly subsides at the thought, forced to make room for the anxiety now rippling through me. There's no tracking my way back. The densely packed underbrush would make it impossible. There's not a single visible footprint.

With no better option, I choose a direction and start the slow trek across the forest. Every snap of a twig has my pulse racing, my eyes scanning for any indication that I'm going the right way. Thoughts of giant bears and wild boar fill my mind.

A figure appears out of nowhere, peeking

between the break of trees, silent as an assassin. I cry out as a hand reaches between the wide trunks, wrapping tightly around my wrist before pulling me back against his chest. Not giving my body the chance to shut down and freeze, I fight with everything I have in me—arms thrashing, body spinning. My hands slap at his arms and face, my fingers curling into claws as they rake through the air, trying to find purchase.

"Calm down, Little Dove." A steady, deep voice brushes against my ear, strong arms wrapping around me.

I know that voice.

The scream in my throat dies, turns to ash, and floats away on a cool mountain breeze.

The heat of his breath tickles my skin, and gooseflesh pebbles my skin. His arm around my waist isn't tight, not like the one holding my arms against my torso. His hand . . . his hand is pressed into my abdomen, his fingers barely brushing my hip bone. Close, so close to the area he watched me touch. His fingers trail across that exposed flesh like he's remembering that moment too.

When I spin to face him again, he allows it, but that hand stays splayed across my flesh, circling my hip now, fingers grazing my open, exposed back.

My breasts lift with each deep inhale and

exhale of breath, my eyes holding his. Neither of us speaks. Not that I would know what to say even if I could form words. Which doesn't seem likely. Not with the way he's peering into my eyes, into my soul. My nipples harden, perking up, bright and eager.

My core tightens with the look he gives me. Predatory and hungry. If he were an animal, he'd be a wolf, and I'd be his prey. The thought doesn't scare me. It excites me. Moisture is pooling between my thighs once again, all sense of self-preservation abandoning me.

I want to be devoured.

Consumed.

His eyes dart to my lips, swollen and plump from the adrenaline still pumping through my veins. My tongue slips out, moistening them, readying them. In some distant part of my soul, I know this man is one twitch away from attacking.

And I welcome it.

Without giving either of us a chance to reconsider, I lean forward and press my lips to his.

weston

chapter seven

LUCY PEERS UP AT ME, the fear that had been in her doe eyes now replaced with desire. She's so fucking sweet. And heaven help me, I want a taste.

My dick hardened the moment I saw her hand tucked between her thighs, her cheeks flushed as she watched the scene unfolding in front of her. When she ran, I followed without thought, told myself I just wanted to make sure she was all right. But the longer I stalked her, the more I wanted her. Her perfectly round ass peeked out from under her short skirt every time she leapt over a log or started up a small incline. I wanted to claim her. Gods be damned, I wanted to sink inside her tight pussy and never leave.

I know she's a virgin. Malcom bitched often

enough about the fact that she wouldn't put out until she graduated. My son's lack of tact and restraint annoyed the hell out of me. I marveled at the thought of being the first cock to slide inside her haven, for her soft flesh to give way to my steel. It's a gift, a wonderous fucking gift she was willing to give him, and he was too stupid to realize it.

All he had to do was wait a few more hours, but no . . . his dick led him right to the first warm hole he could slide into.

That's fine.

Good, even.

He wouldn't have known how to usher her into this new world, anyway. He probably would've rammed straight through her hymen and hurt her.

When I finally caught up to her, it took everything in me not to drag her closer and feast on the flesh she was offering so willingly. Like a lamb to slaughter.

Then she launched herself at me, her warm lips pressing into mine. And the reins snapped.

I pull her against my chest, and her breasts push into me, rising and falling with rapid succession. My cock goes rock hard as her small hands wrap around my biceps then slide to my neck.

Her mouth connects with mine again, her

tongue slipping across my lips, teasing mine. My hands slide down her back to her ass, squeezing. Perfectly round and plump. She moans into my mouth, gasping when I lift her a little and grind my cock against her.

I ease her feet back to the ground and trail my fingers across the soft flesh of her ass. She bows her back, pushing her ass into the air, allowing me easier access to her core. A growl rumbles deep in my throat as I run a finger across her panties. Soaked. They're fucking soaking wet with her desire.

"Are you wet for me, Little Dove?"

She whimpers, her head nodding.

The need to taste her, to sink my tongue in between her folds and lap every drop of moisture from her, overcomes me, but I force myself to slow.

She's untouched.

Primed as she may be, rushing will still hurt her. And the last fucking thing I want to do is cause her pain.

Not from this, anyway.

I trace the curve of her mound one more time, pressing softly against her entrance before pulling my hands away. She quivers with the motion. Fucking quivers in my hands like a bird ruffling her feathers before flight. I pull away from her mouth and place a kiss on her neck, running my tongue across her collarbone and nipping at her shoulder.

Pushing her short tank top up, I pull her bra down, freeing her breast. It fills my palm, small and pert. Another moan breaks free from her throat as I run a callused thumb across her nipple. I do it again. Once. Twice. Then I replace my thumb with my mouth. She arches into me, pressing her breast into my mouth. Her hand fists in the hair at the back of my head and pulls, demanding my mouth to take more.

Her breasts were made to be worshiped.

I am their devout acolyte.

If she were to pull back right now and demand we stop, I could die a happy man knowing I'd given the two perfect globes every ounce of my attention. I suck and lap at them, stroking first one and then the other with my tongue, my teeth.

She pants for air. Moans with desire. And she doesn't ask me to stop.

Her skirt slides down her skin with a gentle pull, her panties following shortly behind. And then she's standing before me, eyes bright with that fire that had been in them earlier. Not smoldering. Burning.

Her cheeks are flushed the color of summer roses.

I stare at her, taking her in, soaking this image up and storing it away so that days, weeks, months from now, I can pull it out and recall every minute detail.

I can't keep my hands off her. Like magnets, they're drawn to the soft flesh of her body. She gazes down, watching as my fingers dance across her stomach and sink lower, savoring the feel of her beneath them.

I run my fingers over the dark curls on her pelvis. Lower still. Her breath hitches when I pass so, so gently over her clit.

I hold my own breath in my lungs, waiting, praying she doesn't run. And then I slide a finger inside her pussy.

It's beyond wet. Drenched. And tight. So fucking tight. I growl again. Or moan.

She doesn't ask me to stop.

Doesn't demand that I remove my hand from her body and cease this torturous exploration.

"I'm going to fuck you, Little Dove. This pussy is going to ache when I'm done."

Her eyes meet mine again as I shove deeper inside her, my finger reaching as far as I dare go.

"Now," she pants, grinding down on my hand,

tightening around my finger, squeezing the circulation off.

I smirk and pull free from her. "Not yet, Little Dove."

Her eyes harden a fraction. She has a fire in her soul and doesn't like the idea of being denied what she wants. The thought of molding that, of bending that stubbornness to my will has my cock twitching, precum coating the band of my jeans.

"You want my cock inside you, Little Dove?" I ask.

She nods her head, her hands reaching for the button on my jeans. I wrap my hands around hers. She pauses, glancing up at me.

"I didn't hear you," I say.

"How would you like me to respond?" She peers up at me with feigned innocence. Oh, yes, breaking her would be a joy. "Should I get on my knees and beg? Or maybe you'd rather a gratifying *yes, Master.*"

I smile down at her, the look anything but gentle and kind. Pulling her closer, I spin her body around and press into her, making sure she understands exactly what she'll be getting when, and only when, I decide to fill her. Her breathing turns ragged. I lean forward, pressing my lips to her neck.

"Lean forward and place your hands against the trunk of that tree."

She follows my command immediately.

"Lower," I grind out and take a step back. Beautiful. She's fucking beautiful. Her ass is in the air, her pussy glistening with the proof of her desire. I run a hand down her spine, then the crack of her ass, all the way through the slit of her pussy, dropping to my knees, and I fucking devour her.

lucy

chapter eight

COOL BRISK AIR fans across the wetness between my thighs, the moisture seeping out of my pussy. My body is tense in anticipation, almost humming with it.

This may not have been the way I saw this weekend going, but I'm not about to balk now. The anger at what Malcom did still coats my veins, and I can't wait to lash into him for it. But right now . . . right now, I don't want to think about Malcom at all. Especially not when his father steps up behind me, running a hand down my spine.

The only thing I want to think about is Weston and that glorious cock I felt in his jeans.

"I'm going to fuck you, Little Dove."

Yes. Yes. Yes. Please. I would beg. Quite literally

beg if that's what he wanted. What he demanded. Anything as long as he fills me.

I'm so focused on my own thoughts I don't realize he's gone silent behind me. I almost turn, almost pull my hands from the trunk of that blasted tree and peer over my shoulder to see him.

Then I feel it.

I feel *him*.

His rough beard grazes the back of my thighs moments, mere moments, before his tongue trails through the slit of my pussy. My knees threaten to buckle. Only sheer will is keeping them locked in place, refusing to fall. He pulls back a fraction and his lips press to my clit, then his magnificent, perfect tongue runs along the slit again.

"Mmm. You taste like heaven."

I don't bother asking what heaven tastes like. Not when his tongue presses to my clit and flicks. Once. Twice. Three times.

"Like honeysuckles and the night sky." His words rumble against my sensitive flesh. I bite back a gasp. Barely.

And then he consumes me.

It takes every ounce of strength to hold myself up and not let go of the tree. It's my lifeline, the only thing anchoring me to this earth as his mouth latches onto my pussy. His lips are soft, feathery soft across my clit when he kisses it.

Lick. Kiss. Lick. Kiss.

His lips close over that sensitive nub and suckle it into his warm, wet mouth. I am floating, careening across the sky, chasing stars as they plummet down, down, down to the earth. My whole body tightens. Ripples.

It starts low in my spine and spreads across my navel. Building. Building. Building.

Crashing.

I'm a shooting star. And finally, after eighteen years of existence, I understand why those stars choose to fly.

My breath is rasping out of my lungs, my legs shaking with the ferocity of the orgasm that rips through me. Never in my life have I felt anything like this. I didn't even know it was possible. Distantly, I wonder if this is how Elisa felt with Malcom between her legs, deciding I really don't care.

I can't.

Not when Weston is standing behind me, pressing something hard between my thighs.

One glance over my shoulder, and I know what it is. Moments ago, I wanted to beg for it. Looking at it now, I don't know how the hell it will fit. He runs the length of his cock through the slit of my pussy, coating the shaft with my juices. Back and forth, over and over, while those tremors fade and that intense flame starts kindling again.

"Did that feel good, Little Dove?"

I moan my yes.

He slides his cock along my slit again then slaps my ass, causing a sharp sting to spread across my cheek.

"I asked you a question," he growls, gently caressing the spot he smacked. I glance over my shoulder again, my eyes meeting his, and grin. His gaze narrows, and his palm slaps my other cheek. Heat floods my face, embarrassment staining it. No, this is something else entirely. Something I don't have a name for yet. He tracks the rose flush with his perceptive gaze as surprise followed quickly with pleasure flits across his face.

"You like that, don't you?" he says, slapping a palm to my ass again. "Oh, Little Dove, we're going to have so much fun."

I don't bother replying. My voice wouldn't work even if I wanted it to. He presses the head of his cock against the entrance to my pussy and slowly pushes in. I brace for pain, knowing it will come. God knows, I've read enough books to know the first time always hurts like a bitch.

I didn't anticipate losing my virginity like this.

My body tenses involuntarily, readying for the initial bite, but it doesn't come.

Weston slides the head of his cock inside me and slowly pulls it back out, rubbing it across my clit before sliding it back inside. Over and over.

My body trembles with fear. With arousal. With anticipation. I want it.

"I need it."

I don't realize I've spoken out loud until he replies, "Tell me. Tell me how badly you need me buried inside you."

I can't. I don't know how. I don't know what words to say and how to say them. I don't know what he wants to hear. So slowly, he pushes inside me, just barely, and pulls back out once again. I groan and rage internally.

"Please," I beg.

"I need it." His cock slides across my clit.

"I want it." He presses inside me.

"All of it," I plead.

That pressure builds inside me once more, demanding that I pay attention, that I stoke those embers into wild, burning flames and let go. His hand reaches around my waist, his fingers deftly coaxing that inferno closer and closer. I moan, my head hanging, my breaths short, panting. His cock flexes inside me, still just the head, but I feel it swell and jump inside me.

That wave is nearly on top of me now, threatening to crash and roar over me.

"Please," I pant, arching my ass for him, begging with every fiber of my being.

He pushes into me.

There's a quick, piercing flash of pain. Sharp and fierce. But then he's in me, fully seated inside. His finger is circling my clit, around and around. He doesn't make a move to slide out. That wave receded a bit when he pressed in, but now it's building again. My veins feel like they're flooding with liquid fire.

"So fucking tight." He grinds into me. His cock's buried so deep I press a hand to my stomach and fully expect to feel him there. His fingers pause, and I want to cry out. *No. Don't stop.* Please don't stop. I'm almost there. I can feel that flutter forming, ready to spread out and explode through my body. I whimper and edge my own hand down my stomach to that sensitive nub.

He pulls my hand away, slides out an inch, then pushes back into me, thrusting his cock home inside me and slapping four fingers across my clit.

I'm too stunned to move. To speak. He

caresses it with gentle fingers, barely trailing across that one spot I so desperately need him to touch.

One breath. Two. And then he smacks my clit again.

The wave stops rolling to a crest. It stops the gentle laps toward shore, and with another stinging slap against my clit, that wave shatters, exploding outward like a tsunami. I scream into the forest with the force of my release, scream until my throat burns and my body heats with the rolling crescendo.

His cock slides out of me and thrusts back in hard and fast, in and out, each stroke sending those waves back up, refusing to let them bank and die out at the shore. Harder and harder, he fucks me. I clench around him, suctioning his cock tighter and tighter with each tremor.

"You like that, Little Dove? Such a good girl."

His hands grip my hips now, squeezing them tightly as he glides that magnificent cock along my insides and slams back into me. My voice is hoarse. I can barely speak, only managing to pant out a single word with every thrust.

"Yes."

"Yes."

"Yes."

With a final thrust, he pulls my hips and grinds

his cock inside me, grinds his pelvis as deep as it will physically go. That spiraling wave reaches higher once more, and when his cock jumps . . . when it pulses inside me, that storm erupts once more.

"Mine. You're mine now, Little Dove."

My pussy clenches around him, sucking, milking every drop.

He leans over my back, presses a kiss between my shoulder blades, and repeats his claim once more. "You're mine."

weston

chapter nine

I SLIDE my cock from her tight sheath with expert gentleness. She moans, light and breathy. Lucy might've been a virgin before today, but that girl was made to be fucked. Her body sang with each stroke, coming alive under my fingers and lips. Just the thought of how she clenched around me has my cock lifting its head once more. I pull my jeans up and tuck it inside.

Bending down, I slide her panties up her silky-smooth thighs, then do the same with her skirt. She stands erect and turns to face me, her eyes looking anywhere but at my own. "You might be a little sore for a while." Her hand runs across her stomach and down between her thighs, testing the flesh. When she pulls away, her fingers are glistening with the proof of our coupling, tinted red with her virginal blood.

"It's not too bad," she says, still avoiding my gaze.

I wrap my hand around her wrist and lift her fingers to my mouth. My tongue darts out, licking the evidence off her. Her eyes shoot to mine then, darkening with desire once more.

"Mmm. So innocent and fucking beautiful."

A blush stains her cheeks, but she doesn't break eye contact until I release her hand. She arranges her skirt and runs her fingers through her hair. The wild curls bounce around her face.

"Come on, let's get you back to the camp so you can clean up."

"Do you know the way? I kinda got turned around."

"Yes. It's not too far. Are you okay to walk?"

"I'm fi—good," she says.

Turning, I start walking. She follows behind me for a few minutes before catching up and walking alongside me. I glance at her from the corner of my eye and can almost see the thoughts spinning in her head.

"I know he's my son, but you're too fucking good for him. I think you already knew that, though, didn't you?"

She pulls on a curl, wrapping it around her finger over and over, before replying, "It was fun, I think. In the beginning, anyway. Then one month turned into two and two into six . . . seven. It got me out of the house and away from my mom, but I knew I didn't love him, knew that it wouldn't last. It doesn't make what he did okay."

"True, but is there a difference between what he did and what we just did?"

"That was . . . that was a reaction. A consequence of his actions. I wouldn't have done that if he didn't . . . if I hadn't caught him like that."

I nod my head in understanding. "I get that. But the fact is, we did. So, what do you plan to do now?"

"Oh, we're so done. He just doesn't know it yet. As soon as we get back, he will."

I let her stew in that anger for the rest of the walk back. Every once in a while, she reaches up and runs a light touch along her lips, as if she's remembering the feel of mine against her. I wish I could put into words how it feels knowing that no other man has ever touched her. No other man has had the pleasure of burying himself in her sensual pink folds, and none will.

That thought shocks me enough to keep me from speaking.

The bathhouse is empty when we arrive. I check the stalls then walk into the shower room and cut on the water. It sprays against the tiled floor in a steady stream. When I come back out, Lucy is pulling her shirt over her head.

Fucking hell, she is the most beautiful creature I've ever laid eyes on.

And right now, she's mine. Only mine. My seed fills her womb, coating her walls on the inside. Stepping closer, I take the shirt from her hands and toss it across a stall door, then run my hands up her back and unlatch her bra. It slides down her arms with ease, freeing her perky tits. They pebble under my scrutiny, begging for my mouth. I don't deny them.

First one and then the other, I take them into my mouth, flicking my tongue across her nipples. Her breath hitches. Her eyes are glazed when I pull away.

"What if you don't say anything to him?"

"What? Why?"

"If you do, then y'all will fight, and I'm sure you'll want to go home. But if you pretend you never saw it, you can stay, and we can have this weekend together." I don't bother telling her that this weekend won't be enough, that I am already imagining her in my bed at home and a hundred other places. No, one weekend will never be enough.

I slide her skirt and panties back down her thighs, kneeling before her and untying the laces of her boots before pulling them off and tossing them aside. I glance up at her fully naked body before me and meet her gaze. "Can you do that?" I ask, running my fingers up her leg, making small circles across her thighs before brushing against her dripping apex.

"Why?" The question is a breathless whisper.

She's completely bared to me, her body soft and supple, mine for the taking. I lower my hungry mouth and apply pressure to her welcoming folds. She tastes like honeysuckles and sweet red wine. I lick slowly, tasting, teasing. Her pussy is drenched with need and the proof of our prior coupling. The coppery tang of blood from where my cock tore through her virginal veil is mixed with the sinful sweetness of her desire. I lap it up like a kitten before a bowl of milk.

"Because I want to spend the weekend worshiping your body. When I finish, you won't be able to sit or walk without remembering just how far I stretched that tight pussy around my cock."

Unbuttoning my jeans, I pull the front open.

My cock pops free. I stroke it as I fuck her deca-
dent pussy with my tongue. She leans against the
sink counter and places one leg on my shoulder.
God, what I would do to lay her in a bed and fuck
her properly. She wouldn't be able to walk for days.
I'd tie her up and keep her there, my willing
prisoner.

I nibble her clit and then suckle it into my
mouth, flicking my tongue across it. Her legs
quake. "Do you want to come, Little Dove?"
Close, so fucking close.

She nods, and I pause, looking up at her. "Yes.
Please." I press a finger to the soaked entrance of
her pussy and slowly push inside her. My dick
twitches with the need to bury myself in her again.
I stroke one hand up and down its length while
pumping fingers of the other inside her and press
my mouth back to her center.

"Oh, shit." Her hand twists my hair as her
pussy clenches around my fingers. I release her clit
and gently press my tongue to it, easing her down
from the orgasm slowly. When her leg falls from
my shoulder, I stand and pull free from her folds.
Lifting my hand, I suck her juices off my fingers
and then press my mouth to hers, letting her taste
herself on my tongue.

Her hand reaches for my cock, her delicate

fingers wrapping around it. She strokes up and down its length while her tongue explores my mouth. She pulls away and drops to her knees in front of me. I stare down at her, watching as her tongue darts out and licks the tip of my cock. It jumps against her hand, and she grins before doing it again. I tilt my head back, groaning at her teasing.

She presses her lips to the side of my cock and alternates between kissing and licking up the length of it. When she makes her way back to the tip, she opens her mouth and wraps her lips around the head. My hips jerk forward, wanting to bury myself balls deep in her throat. I fight the urge to fuck her mouth and let her have control.

She eases my dick in, inch by inch. Her mouth is as soft and sweet as her pussy. Her tongue wraps around my cock as she swallows more of me, and then her hand joins, wrapping around the base of my dick and sliding up the shaft in time with the movements of her mouth. When she reaches the head again, she creates suction and flicks her tongue on the underside of the head.

I fist her hair and hold her head in place. "Open for me, baby."

Her lips spread, her mouth opening wider. I thrust my hips forward until my cock reaches the back of her throat. Her eyes water, but she doesn't stop me. I fuck her mouth, thrusting in and out of the warm haven. My balls tighten. I shove to the back of her throat and grind my cock there, rubbing the head on the silky flesh. With a groan, my cock jerks and squirts down her throat. She swallows every drop.

I pull her to my chest and press a kiss to her brow bone, her cheek, then her lips. "Such a good girl. Now go clean up while I start the grill for dinner."

Righting myself and my jeans, I walk outside. It's hard as fuck to leave her there, but I know Malcom and Elisa will be back soon, if they aren't already, and I don't feel like dealing with questions right now. I want to keep this a secret, not because I'm ashamed. Far from it. I don't give a fuck who knows, but I like this game. It's exciting and fun.

Besides, it's not like Mal isn't keeping his own fair share of secrets.

lucy

chapter Ten

STEPPING INTO THE SHOWER, I let the events of the last few hours wash over me. It's definitely been the strangest day of my entire life and nothing like I had originally planned. Obviously. I don't know many women who imagine their boyfriend sleeping with his stepsister or follow up that betrayal by fucking his dad.

Not that I regret it one bit. Weston is . . . he's everything I ever fantasized he would be. I can still feel the scruff of his five-o clock shadow on the inside of my thighs, his lips pressed to my clit.

Tilting back my hair, I rinse, letting the soapy suds wash down my body and out the drain. Grabbing a bar of soap, I lather it in my hands and run them across my flesh, taking special care to cleanse between my legs. I'm swollen and tender, but in the best possible way.

When I step from the shower, the bath house is still empty, but on the counter is a pile of fresh clothes. Smiling, I dry off and slip into the loose shorts and tee. The sun has almost fully set, a few pinks and purples spreading along the horizon.

Stepping toward the blazing fire, I meet Weston's stare and a blush coats my cheeks.

"Finally, a woman. Please tell me you know how to cook. I don't know if I can take another burnt hotdog," Carson says as I join them.

I chuckle. "You could always eat it raw."

He mimics holding his chest while another friend of Weston's laughs. "Baby, you wound me."

I've just sat down when Malcom and Elisa come walking up. The urge to jump up and confront him right here is almost more than I can fight. I glance at Weston, who seems to be waiting to see how I'll handle it, when Malcom reaches my side. He leans in, trying to plant a kiss on my lips, but I jerk back and narrow my eyes. The words are on the tip of my tongue, begging for release.

"Babe?"

"Don't call me babe. Actually, don't speak to me at all," I say, standing and walking toward the tent. He follows me, trying to grab my hand.

Crossing them over my chest, I turn and glare at him. "You have a lot of nerve, walking back up here like you didn't abandon me for hours."

"I lost track of time and we got turned around. I'm sorry."

As lies go, that one isn't even well thought out. It shows exactly how much I matter to him. A part of me wonders how long this thing has been going on between them and how I could be so stupid and blind.

"I don't care what lame ass excuse you have. The fact is that you ran off without even asking whether I wanted to come. You left me here for hours alone." I don't have to pretend the anger I feel toward him, even if I'm choosing not to disclose the real reason behind it. Fake it until you make it, right?

"You weren't alone. My dad is here. I knew you were fine."

I chuckle dryly. He has no idea just how fine I was with his dad.

"That's not the fucking point," I grind out.

"What do you want me to say?"

"What were you doing? Where did you go?" This is it, the last chance he has to tell me the truth. At this point, I would accept any version of it, just not outright lies.

"I told you, I wanted to show Elisa this cool rock formation I found the last time I was here. She's into that stuff."

"Right. And I'm not? You didn't think I'd want to see it?"

"Babe, come on. I can take you tomorrow if you really wanna see it." Running a hand through his hair, he turns pleading eyes on me. Before today, it might have worked. But that was before.

"I'll pass. I already made plans."

He doesn't try to stop me as I storm past him. When I reach my seat again, Weston just raises his brows in question. I shake my head no. No, I didn't confront him on the cheating. I'll keep my mouth shut for now, if for no other reason than I kind of like this little game. And when it's over, we'll see how he feels with betrayal shoved down his throat.

I hope he fucking chokes on it.

Malcom doesn't approach me again. And it's a good thing. I don't think I could swallow the words I really want to say again if he kept trying to justify his actions. After a few minutes, my racing heart slows to a more normal pace. Conversation around me carries on normally, which seems so strange.

"Here, asshole. Cook your own food if you're so worried about it burning."

"What do you expect me to do with this, Ash? Stab my prey?" Carson asks, holding up a skewer.

"No, dumbass. You stick the hot dog on it and hold it over the flame."

"How was I supposed to know that? Do I look like a caveman to you?" He seems to rethink that and backtracks. "On second thought, don't answer that. Give me a weenie."

"I'll give you a weenie," Pacey says, shoving his crotch into Carson's face with an overexaggerated thrust.

"Don't threaten me with a good time, big boy."

"Want it? Take it, Daddy."

The whole thing is so overdramatic and outlandish that I can't keep a straight face.

I almost tip my chair back laughing so hard. My stomach aches, and the muscles in my cheeks feel like they're going to split when Carson tosses down his skewer and tackles Pacey to the ground. His hands roam all over Pacey's body while he roars, "Give me that weenie. It's my weenie, and I want it now!"

Somehow, Pacey manages to get away from Carson and picks up the discarded skewer, brandishing it like a sword. I glance at Weston only to find him watching me, a devilish smirk tilting his lips. The space between us tightens with awareness, my pussy throbbing awake once again.

Hiding my attraction to Weston has never been easy, but after today it's become damn near impossible. A part of me wants to throw caution to the wind and wrap my body around him right now. I don't know where this, whatever it is, will go with us. For all I know, I could just be a conquest for him, but I damn sure plan to follow it through to the end and enjoy every second.

weston

chapter eleven

STANDING AROUND THE FIRE, I watch the flames dance through the air. Lucy went into the tent about an hour ago, and every second since she disappeared inside, I've fought the urge to follow her. Malcom and Elisa followed her a few minutes later. Since no one came storming out, I assume Lucy held her tongue and didn't confront him.

The thought fills me with pride. When they came back, I just knew she was going to snap on him. But she held it together.

Fucking hell. I still can't believe I didn't know they were fucking. I should have. Now that I've seen it, it seems so obvious. I still don't know what to do about it, if anything.

"Dude, Earth to Wes." Ash waves his hand in front of my face.

"What?"

"Damn, man, where did you go?"

"I'm tired as fuck. Think I'm gonna crash. I'll see y'all in the morning."

Slipping inside the tent, I shine my light to see where everyone is lying. Malcom is between Elisa and Lucy on his back. The only open spot is right beside Lucy, like she planned for me to slip in next to her. I shuck off my shoes and ease next to her before shutting off my phone's flashlight. She's curled on her side, her legs cradled one on top of the other, facing Malcom, her curls forming a halo around her face.

At some point, she must've gotten hot, or maybe she just fell asleep on top of the cover rather than chancing it. I uncurl a light linen blanket and toss it over us before propping my arms behind my head and closing my eyes.

We're so close I can smell the shampoo in her hair. My hands ache to touch her delicate skin, along with my cock. Turning on my side, I run a finger down her arm and in a gentle circle across her hip. Her breathing is slow and steady. She's sound asleep. A quick glance over at Malcom and Elisa confirms they are as well.

Holding my breath, I run a finger along the hem of her shorts. Her hand lifts to brush mine away, but her back arches inward, seeking. Scooting closer to her, I grind my dick against the swell of her ass while skimming my fingers across every open available piece of flesh. Her breath speeds up, signaling her waking. One second, she's lying still, and the next, her head lifts. She notices Malcom first and then peers over her shoulder. Her darkened, lust-filled eyes meet mine.

"Wes..."

"Shh," I whisper, sliding my finger under the leg of her shorts. She's bare beneath. I didn't see a point in grabbing her panties when I dropped off clothes earlier, and it looks like she didn't mind.

Lying back down, she lifts her hips while tugging at her shorts. I help her, slipping them down far enough that she can kick them off.

One of her legs slides forward, her knee now pressed to the ground for support as she pushes her ass into the air. My fingers run over her swollen lips and up the crease of her ass before retracing the path once again. She's wet already, her juices coating the lips of her pussy.

I inch closer to her and slip my arm under her head. My lips land on the hollow of her neck, nipping the sensitive skin. I run a finger through her slit, gently probing her tight hole.

Her moan lights my blood on fire.

"So wet for me, Little Dove. You like when I touch this pussy, don't you?"

She nods against my arm.

"Can you be quiet for me?" I ask, pushing a finger inside her.

Her answer is a breathy *yes*, and that's all I need.

"I'm going to bring your body to the edge, then I'm going to slide my cock inside you and push you over. Does that sound good?"

Adding a second finger, I push in deep and curl my fingers inside her, back and forth. Her pussy grips me tightly, and I know she's close. My dick jumps in my jeans, begging to be buried inside her.

I pull my fingers free and rub her juices up and down her slit, circling her clit before trailing across her puckered hole. Her hips twitch, thrusting with each swipe, but she doesn't make a peep. I kiss my way down her neck and across her shoulder, then around her back, as low as I can go without pulling away from her. I sink my teeth into her flesh between kisses, marking her body as mine.

Her hand reaches behind her and palms me through my jeans, then tugs at the waistband until I slip them down. My cock bounces free, but her hand is there to catch it. I get lost in the feel of her as she strokes up and down my length, squeezing tighter with each pass.

I almost nut right there. Only years of self-control keep me from losing it completely.

Grabbing her hand, I remove it and then pull her hips toward me. Wrapping a hand around my cock, I slide it between her thighs and along her clit. She clenches her legs, angling her hips trying to get me inside her, but I like this game and I'm not ready for it to end.

I flex my hips back and forth as my cock glides along her slit, her juices coating it more with every swipe. Her hips grind in perfect rhythm to my thrust, each of us chasing a sensuous melody.

"Wes, I . . ."

Angling my arm under her, I cover her mouth, silencing her words. She groans and spreads her lips, licking along my fingers. With my free hand, I grab the base of my cock and tilt it up, pressing against her opening. One push. That's all it would take to bury myself deep inside her.

Beside her, Malcom groans in his sleep and

rolls on his side, facing her. I pause, waiting to see if he'll waken, but a few moments later, his soft snores fill the tent. Lucy's teeth graze my fingers, impatient and demanding. I release her mouth and slide my hand down her neck and around her throat, shoving inside her with a deep thrust.

lucy

chapter Twelve

WESTON'S HAND is tight against my throat as he shoves home inside me. My body is so tightly coiled, ready to explode any minute. Every time I get close, he pauses and makes me start all over. Now, it's all I can do to be silent while he brings my body to heights it's never seen before.

The sounds of our flesh meeting fill the tent, each thrust echoing against the walls. I watch Malcom, hyper focused on his closed eyes while Weston fucks me.

The fact that he could wake at any moment fills me with an alluring excitement. This is more than fucking his dad. This is dirty and hot and fucking thrilling. My pussy tightens as I crest, my nipples hardening. As if he can sense how close I am, Weston tightens his fingers against my neck.

His face is buried in my hair, nuzzling, searching. Moments later, his lips find the skin of my shoulder and trail along the length of my neck. I slip a hand behind my back and dig my fingers into his hip, pulling his body toward mine faster . . . faster.

Then his teeth are buried in the soft the flesh where my neck meets my shoulder. The white-hot pain barely registers as I rush over the edge, clenching around his cock. He thrusts forward, his hand gripping my hip as he follows, filling me with pump after pump of his hot cum.

After a few moments, Weston releases me, slipping his cock free and rolling onto his back. He pulls me with him, then we are both panting, staring at the ceiling of the tent.

He turns back to his side, tracing a finger down my stomach and across my sensitive clit before passing through my slit. When his hand reappears, his fingers are glistening with our combined juices. He presses the fingers to my lips. I open, and he slips them in my mouth. The taste of us is salty and sweet. It's beyond erotic, licking myself from his fingers. I wrap my lips around them and suck them clean.

When he pulls them away, his lips press to mine, his tongue invading my mouth. My fingers dig into his biceps until he slips from my mouth and slides between my thighs. Pushing my legs apart, he presses his lips to my pussy entrance and slips his tongue inside.

Within minutes, my breathing is ragged, my pulse thrumming in my ears once again. How this man manages to make my body react to his touch this way, I may never know. And as long as he doesn't ever stop, I don't care. Weston sucks the lips of my pussy into his mouth, holding the suction while he rolls the flesh with his tongue. When he reaches my clit, he flicks against the sensitive nub over and over again, never once releasing the pressure.

My legs shake uncontrollably. My eyes squeeze shut, blocking out everything but the feel of his mouth on me. His teeth graze me, and my hips thrust up involuntarily, his name a silent scream on my lips as he repeats the gesture again, scraping them gently across me before suckling my flesh back into his mouth.

Light explodes behind my eyelids, stars sparking to life around me as I come fiercely. The tremors quake through my body like a magnitude-eight earthquake.

Weston lifts first one foot and then the other, slipping my shorts back up my thighs. Reaching for the waistband, I pull them up and then fall back on the sleeping bag. He kisses a path back up my body, his lips seeking mine in the dark. I open for him and breathe in the scent of my arousal on his face.

"You taste like heaven, Little Dove. I don't think I'll ever get enough of you."

And then he lies beside me, pulling my head into the crook of his arm. I'm asleep in minutes, my body thoroughly sated.

weston

chapter Thirteen

IT'S hard as hell to crawl from the tent this morning. Lucy is snuggled into my side, burrowed in the warmth of my body. She fits against me like a glove. It shouldn't feel this good, this right. After two failed marriages, I never thought I'd find someone who held my attention and made me want a relationship, but Lucy isn't like any woman I've ever known. She makes me want to live, not just exist. Her goodness shines from her with an internal flame that I can't look away from.

The first rays of sunlight are peeking across the sky when I step from the tent. Pacey is already by the grill, stoking a flame to life for coffee. I pull a chair up and wait for the pot of water to heat. Malcom peeks his bleary-eyed head out thirty minutes later as I'm pouring my first cup. It's been hard as hell to not call him on the shit with Elisa. But in the end, he's a grown ass man and able to make his own decisions.

I'm not even mad about it, honestly. It's the fact that he's strung Lucy along for the ride that really sets my blood boiling. And until yesterday, she had no idea either.

Speak of the devil. Lucy looks adorable as fuck this morning with fresh just-fucked hair and a flush to her cheeks as her eyes meet mine. "Is that coffee I smell?"

"Hot and fresh. Want a cup?" Pacey says, pressing down on the carafe, soaking the roasted beans in hot water.

"I'd kill for one. Literally. Line up your foes." Her mouth opens on a yawn, her arms stretching high overhead.

"No killing required. Have a seat and I'll pour you a cup." He winks, reaching for another mug.

As she passes Malcom, he wraps a hand around her wrist and pulls her into his lap. "I saved you the perfect seat, babe." Her body is tense, and when her gaze meets mine, I can see the struggle playing out behind her eyes. Until now, she's managed to keep her distance from him, to avoid his touch, but now she's stuck and doesn't know what to do. The alarm is written all over her face. It makes me want to step in and pull her from his arms, especially when his hand starts caressing up and down her silken thigh.

She squirms in his arms, pushing against his chest, "Uh . . . nature's calling."

He doesn't immediately release her, choosing instead to nuzzle his face into her hair and along her neck.

"Unless you want me to pee in your lap, you need to let me go."

When Lucy is far enough away, I turn to Malcom, pinning him with a stare. This ends now. If I'm forced to watch him touch her one more second, I'm afraid of what I may do. Already, the sight of her struggling against his hands on her body has me seeing red.

"Do not touch her again. That's enough. She's not a pawn in some sick, twisted game."

"What are you talking about? She's my girl-friend. I'll touch her whenever I want."

"No, you won't. You won't lay a finger on her ever again."

"And why is that?"

"Do you think I'm stupid? I know about you and Elisa. I know about it all. When I say that your relationship with Lucy is over, I mean it."

His face blanches, all color leaking away. His mouth opens and then closes repeatedly before he stands and races back inside the tent. I glance at Pacey, who's just watched everything in silence. "Not a word."

"Me? I'm Switzerland. Count me out."

Satisfied, I take the cup of coffee from Pacey's hand and go to find Lucy. She might be pissed. I didn't even think of that, but it's for the best. She's mine now, and it's about time everyone else knows it too.

As I round the corner of the bathhouse, I hear someone screaming. It takes a second for me to realize Lucy is on the phone. I pause to give her time to finish the call, but it's hard not to overhear the conversation

"How could you do that? Because of you, I'm going to lose everything. You're such a lying, ungrateful brat. You need to apologize right now."

"I will not apologize. I did nothing wrong."

"You lied. Roger would never touch you. I've seen the way you watch him. I know you want him."

Lucy scoffs. *"I watch him because he gives me the creeps. Every time I walk in the room, he grabs his dick, Mom."*

Fucking hell. This is her mother? This is the shit she deals with at home? I don't know who

Roger is, but if I ever run into the sonofabitch, he won't have eyes left to watch her with.

"You will apologize to him and mean it. He's packing his things right now, refusing to stay here with someone who flings such baseless accusations."

"Good riddance."

"No. I won't lose him because you're a little slut, teasing him. You either apologize or don't bother coming back."

"You're really going to choose him over your own daughter? You know what? Never mind. I won't be back."

Thirty seconds. I'll give her thirty seconds before going to her so she doesn't know I overheard. Counting in my head, I make it to seventeen before the sound of her sobs reaches me. Rushing inside, I find her leaning over the counter, one arm gripping her stomach, her head bowed on the other across the counter.

"Lucy."

She jerks back, her hands swiping at her face, but the tears don't quit flowing.

"I . . . I'm so s—sorry."

"What happened?" Setting the cup of coffee on the counter, I pull her into my arms. She buries her face in her hands and presses them both to my chest. I trace a hand up and down her back in soothing circles while she attempts to calm her breathing.

"She just . . . how could she do this?" Her words are broken between sobs she is fighting to keep inside.

"Tell me what happened. Who hurt you, Little Dove?" I ask, trying my best to remain calm when every instinct is telling me to get in my truck and drive to her mother's house right now.

She pulls away abruptly, reaching for a rough paper towel. "Nothing. I'm fi—"

"Don't you dare say fine. Tell me." I growl out the last word.

"It's nothing you need to concern yourself with. I'll handle it."

Wrapping my hand around her shoulder, I spin her around and tilt her head, forcing her to look me in the eye. Nothing about this shit is okay, and I'm sick of pretending otherwise. This girl has gotten under my skin and burrowed into my fucking soul. She needs to understand that.

"Do you think this was just fun for me? A quick fuck over a weekend? You are mine, Little Dove, and someone has hurt you. That means you will tell me, and we will handle it together. Do you understand?"

She nods, wide-eyed.

"Good. Start at the beginning."

"I was getting ready for the party Friday, and the bathroom was hot, so I opened the door while I finished my hair. Roger . . . Roger is my mom's boyfriend. He's been staying there for a few weeks."

I nod in understanding and wait for her to continue.

"Anyway, I was almost done when he walked past then backtracked and pushed inside the bathroom. I yelled at him to leave, but he ignored me and started reaching for me. One hand grabbed my . . . it squeezed my boob . . . while the other one groped at my crotch. I yelled at him to stop and kneed him between the legs. When he fell, he was shouting and screaming at me. My mom ran in, and I told her what happened, but Roger just kept calling me a lying cunt.

"What did your mom do?"

"She flipped out . . . *on me,* yelling about how I should be ashamed while she helped him to his feet, and I just fled."

"When you walked inside, you were upset. This had just happened."

She nods. Pulling her back into my arms, I press my cheek to the top of her head. "You're not going back there. When we leave here, you're coming home with me. I don't want you to step foot back inside that house ever again."

"My clothes . . ."

"We'll get you new clothes. Anything you need. But you don't look back. Deal?"

I don't bother telling her that it's safer this way. If she went back there, I would be by her side, and I don't trust myself to not touch Roger inappropriately myself. A fist to the nose, for example. The idea of him putting his hands on her, trying to force her into something she didn't fully consent to . . . I'll kill the motherfucker. No one touches what is mine.

lucy

chapter fourteen

TEN MINUTES LATER, sitting around the fire pit, the thoughts rushing through my mind have slowed and I've somewhat accepted the fact that Weston wants me. I mean, I knew he wanted me physically. The chemistry between us can't be denied. But he wants more. I don't know exactly how much more, and right now, it doesn't really matter. One day at time.

The relief at knowing I never have to go back to my mother's house . . . God. I can't even describe how it feels.

I pinch my skin just to make sure I'm not dreaming. A pink circle forms on my skin. Weston reaches over and rubs the tender spot with the pad of his finger before pulling me close and pressing his lips to mine. Everything around fades to background noise when he touches me, and my body awakens. I lose myself in that kiss, in the feel of his soft lips pressed to mine, his tongue dancing with my own. Even the guys' whistling across the pit gets drowned out by the raging beat of my heart.

"Oh, so this is how it is?" Malcom says, standing just a foot away with his arms crossed across his chest. I jump as Weston pulls back and straightens. "This is why you told me to leave her alone? And you, I guess any man will do, huh?"

"Really? You want to do this?" I grind out, noting the guys watching the show out of my peripheral.

"Do what? Call out my slut of a girlfriend? What a fucking joke. I should've known you were worthless. Trailer trash, just like your junkie of a mother."

His words hit me like a brick, so similar to the hateful comments my mother spewed at me. Only this time, they don't hurt. My heart doesn't shatter, pieces falling to ground and scattering. No, now all I feel is anger. It courses through me, flooding my veins. My vision tunnels, the edges blackening. He has the nerve, the audacity to say something to me while he's been fucking his stepsister for who knows how long. He chose to ruin this relationship long before I realized I didn't want *him*.

"That's enough, Malcom. We both know you have no room to talk." Weston growls the last word, a sinful edge to his tone.

"Fuck you."

The roaring settles, all sound cut off like the calm in the middle of a tornado. Distantly, I know I shouldn't open my mouth, shouldn't let my anger unfurl into piercing words thrown with unnerving accuracy, but in this moment, I don't care.

Malcom spins on his heel, and for a second, I think it's over, that he's going to walk away and let it go, but he turns, his gaze meeting mine. "We are so done. I can't believe I wasted seven months on a fucking lying whore. Seven months waiting to fuck you when you're more than happy to spread those legs for anyone."

"Oh, Malcom, you're *so* right. You hit the nail on the head, and it only took you seven long months to figure me out. Tell me, do you think your dad's cum tastes as good as your sister's?"

"Oh, shit," Carson singsongs across the fire pit.

Malcom's eyes round, his gaze darting between me and his dad. I lift a finger and wipe at the corner of my mouth. "A little sweet, with just a hint of saltiness, if you ask me."

"You motherfucker," he says, moments before storming toward Weston. I sidestep out of the way while Asher and Pacey move to stop him, but Weston waves a hand, and they back away.

Elisa chooses that moment to walk back up, and judging by the shocked expression on her face, this isn't something that occurs often. Malcom raises an arm and swings, but Weston moves to the left, and he hits nothing but air.

"You don't want to do this, Malcom. You know you don't want this. Be happy with what you do have and let Lucy go."

"You fucked her. That was mine," he says, spinning back around, his fist flying once again. This time, Weston catches it in his hand and stops the swing in motion. Using Malcom's own fist, he pushes him backward step after step.

"She was never yours. You made that choice when you started fucking Elisa. Now grow up and accept the consequences of your own fuckups."

When Weston releases his hand, Malcom stumbles back and trips. One second, he's standing and the next, he's flat on his back, staring up at the blue sky. Shaking my head, I move as far away from him as possible and sit in the chair next to Asher.

Weston pulls one over and slides it next to mine. Taking my hand in his, he raises my knuckles to his mouth and presses a gentle kiss there.

"So, um . . . you guys?" Asher starts, but a glare from Weston shuts him up.

"I'm just saying . . . congrats. I think."

"Fuck off, Ash."

He holds his hands in the air, palms out. "I'm happy for you, man. That's all."

"Ditto. Now how about you tell me where I can find me one?" Carson says, picking up a discarded chair and sitting.

"Me too. Don't leave me out." Pacey seconds the sentiment. Laughter bubbles out, covering the horror of what they're saying. A few minutes ago, I was afraid Malcom and Weston were going to come to blows, and now these guys are sitting here discussing picking up women. Men confuse me.

Weston chuckles. "Shut up. You have enough women."

"One never has enough women."

"You only need one. You just need to find her." His eyes meet mine, his lips tilting up in that devilish smirk.

weston

chapter fifteen

LYING ON MY BACK, I pull Lucy to my chest and inhale her sweet scent. Carson gave Malcom and Elisa his tent, which means he's bunking with us tonight. And being loud as hell. I swear, he has rolled ten times in the last five minutes, huffing and puffing each time. "Can you be still?" I growl.

"Shit, man, I'm trying to get comfortable," he grumbles.

"Try harder," I growl into the dark. "I need sleep."

I don't let my hands stray past Lucy's bra strap. The moment I do, I know I won't be able to stop. She's like an addiction, one I don't think I'll ever give up. I'll be damned if I share an inch of her with Carson's prying eyes. He hasn't stopped flirting with her since the moment he met her.

Pressing a kiss to her head, I shut my eyes and force myself to relax.

The next time I open them, it's morning and Lucy is shifting in the pallet next to me.

"Morning."

Her answering smile could light the world on fire. There's an openness in her eyes now that wasn't there before, and I don't know if it's because I claimed her or because she doesn't have to worry about going home. I don't really care as long as those shadows never creep back in.

"You ready to head home?" I ask, nuzzling her neck.

"Sorta. I kinda wish we didn't have to leave at all," she says with a sigh.

"Hmm."

Standing up, I pull her to her feet, and together, we step from the tent. Pacey is loading his truck up already. "You getting ready to head out?"

"Yeah, just waiting on Ash to get his shit together and we're hitting the road," he says, tossing a bag into the cab.

"You think Carson will let Malcom ride back with him?" I ask.

"Will Carson what? I know I heard my name."
Speak of the devil and he will appear.

Turning back to the tent entrance where
Carson is emerging rubbing his eyes, I ask him,
"You wanna let Malcom ride back with you?"

He stares for a moment, like he's piecing the
words together, before nodding his head. "Yeah,
and Elisa too. I'll drop her at Maggie's. Where do I
need to take Malcom?"

"That's up to him."

"Got it. Y'all enjoy the ride back in peace. But
you owe me for this one," he says, grinning from
ear to ear.

"Owe *you?* Last I checked, you still owe me for
taking What's-Her-Name home and pretending
you got called into work." It takes a second, but
when he remembers, his eyes widen.

"Damn, man, that's fucked up. We said we
would never speak of it again."

"We won't." I chuckle. "Now we're even.
Thanks, man."

lucy

chapter sixteen

THE IDEA STARTS FORMING in my mind while Weston works out the details with Carson. It takes everything in me not to give myself away.

But then everyone is loaded up, and we're the only two left watching the guys' trucks kick up dust down the dirt road.

Pulling my hand from Weston's, I start slowly walking backward. He spins to face me. "What are you doing?"

Lifting the hem of my shirt, I tug it over my head and toss it on the ground while steadily putting more space between us.

Weston cocks his head to the side and takes a step toward me. "Lucy . . ."

I pop the button on my shorts free and pull the zipper down. Pausing, I kick off my Birkenstocks and slide my shorts off, never taking my eyes off Weston's.

He grins devilishly, and my pulse skyrockets, my heart fighting against my ribcage to burst free. When he lunges after me, I spin and run down the pier. For a second, I'm flying, nothing touching my skin but hot air, then I'm falling, falling, falling.

My feet break the water, my body sinking until I touch the murky bottom. Then I'm pushing up, up, up. Weston is there when I break the surface, his arms circling my waist and holding me afloat in the water.

One minute, I'm catching my breath and the next, he's pressing inside me, filling me, and the air whooshes right back out. Wrapping my arms around his neck, I hold tight to him as he thrusts in and out. His thumbs dig into my hips, his fingers pressing firmly into my ass with each pass.

My orgasm rips through without warning. Weston buries his head in my neck, his lips pressed to my beating artery. "Fuck, your pussy is so fucking tight." He groans, "Hold on tight, Little Dove."

I lift my head, opening my eyes for the first time since my body exploded around him. The weightless feel of the water slowly dissipates with each step closer to the bank, then he is laying me down on soft grass and lifting my legs to his shoulders.

When he slides back inside me, the feeling is unlike anything I have ever felt before. I'm beyond full, heavy with his cock deep inside me. He glances down, watching himself sliding out agonizingly slowly.

"I love watching your pussy spread for me. You feel me stretching you?" He pushes back inside. "You're so fucking wet. That pussy knows what it needs."

"Ye–Yes," I stutter around a breath as he pulls back and thrusts inside again.

Leaning forward, he lifts my ass into the air, my legs so close to my face I could turn my head and kiss them. "This is mine."

"*Yes!*" The word is a scream pulled from my chest.

He growls. "Say it."

"It's yours." I moan the words, unable to fight the storm building in my veins. My core tightens, a sensation building deep in my stomach and spiraling faster and faster.

Pressing a hand to each side of my head for support, he slides in and out of me, his flesh slapping against mine over and over. "Again."

The storm is about to erupt. My vision darkens, stars bursting to light all around. "It's yours. Only yours."

"Good girl. Now come for me."

I shatter.

three years later

pacey

epilogue

LEANING my head against the wall, I try to block out the raging music blasting through the bar. People come here to eat. They could at least keep the volume down until after dinner.

Lifting my phone, I check it for the hundredth time in the last ten minutes, but there are no new messages. I don't know how to do this shit. I'm not a whiny bitch who falls for someone after the first hookup. I'm the guy who walks away.

I don't do relationships. Never have and never will.

So why the fuck is this chick getting to me?

We had a good time. At least I thought we did. And then when we finished, she stood up, grabbed a towel, and tossed my clothes to me with a dry, *"You remember where the door is, right? Don't be here when I come back out."*

I was too stunned to do anything other than get dressed and leave.

It's been three fucking weeks and I haven't heard a peep from her. Today, I finally got up the nerve to call her, but it went straight to voicemail, so I followed it up with a text inviting her out tonight.

Glancing at my phone again, I open up Messages. Nothing. Zilch. Nada. Closing out of that app, I text Ash just to make sure the fucking thing works.

"Dude, did you just text me WYD? You know I'm sitting right here next to you."

"Fuck off. I know that. I was just checking my phone."

"Aw, leave him alone, Ash. You know he doesn't know what to do with all these feelings," Lucy says, striding up to the table. It's her twenty-first birthday, and when Weston asked her what she wanted to do, this is what she came up with.

All of us here, at the bar where she first met Weston. Her eyes light up with mirth, and if I weren't in such a shit mood, I'd pick back at her. But this chick has me all out of sorts. I don't know up from down or left from right anymore.

It's fucking pathetic.

"Harriet still hasn't reached out?" Lucy asks,

her gaze narrowing on the phone clutched in my hand.

"Not a fucking word," I grunt out.

"Maybe she died," Weston offers, joining the conversation.

"She didn't fucking die, you sick fuck." The words are barked out.

He shrugs, turning up his beer. "She could have. I mean, what other woman would ignore you this long? You tried to call her?" he asks.

"Yes. And I messaged her. But I know she isn't dead. She posted to social media yesterday," I say, twirling my bottle on the table.

"Jesus, Pace, you're cyberstalking her?" Lucy gasps, shocked.

"No. Yes? Fuck, I don't know what I'm doing." Placing my head in my hands, I rub my forehead. When did my life get so twisted?

The guys all laugh at my expense, but Lucy's eyes fill with sympathy. And isn't that just fucking great.

"I know how to make her stop ignoring you, but you might not like it," she offers, her tone edged with a wicked delight.

I practically leap in my seat at the chance. "How? Tell me."

"Hand me your phone," she says before

standing on her tiptoes and whispering something in Weston's ear. He grins and nods.

Eyeing her warily, I pass her my phone. She opens the camera app and checks her reflection in the screen. After adjusting her top to show way more cleavage than I need to see, she slides between my legs, her back pressed against my chest, and holds the camera high.

"Smile or nuzzle my hair and pretend like you're having the time of your life."

"What?" I ask, almost positive I heard her wrong, but she just stares at me, waiting.

"Just do it."

I follow her direction and try not to flinch when she turns her face toward mine and presses her lips to my cheek. She snaps a few pics and then mercifully steps away. Glancing to Weston, I brace myself, but he just smiles and slaps my shoulder.

After a few minutes, Lucy passes my phone back, a wicked grin gracing her face. "If she doesn't text within ten minutes, write her off. But I'd bet my left tit that she is stalking you as much as you are her and she will—"

She doesn't even get the chance to finish the sentence before his phone vibrates on the counter. I stare in wonder as Harriet's name flashes across the top. I reach for it, but Lucy lays a hand on top of mine, stopping me.

"Not yet. Let her sweat it out," she says, grinning.

"What the hell did you do?" I can't fucking believe it. Less than a minute. That's all it took.

"It's the oldest trick in the book. I just made her think you had moved on." Opening her own phone, she pulls up my Instagram, and right there for the world to see is Lucy in my arms with the caption, *hacked by your number one* with two heart emoticons.

Damn. I shake my head. Picking up my phone, I slip it in my back pocket and take a swig of my beer. So far, everything Lucy has done has worked, so if she says let her sweat it out, then I'll leave her in a puddle.

Not how I wanted her attention, but I can't deny there is a sick satisfaction to be had knowing she was stalking me as much as I was her. I knew it. Now I just need to figure out how to play this, and more importantly, why we're playing a game at all.

One thing is for certain. Regardless of the whos, whats, and whys, I will win this game. And when I have her, she'll wish she'd never started playing at all.

PACEY'S STORY

Pacey's book is coming soon and it is already hotttter than Weston and Lucy's story.
To preorder it now click here

acknowledgements

THIS BOOK HAS BEEN a work of passion. The concept came to me with one line, and quickly grew from there. Thank you for reading it and taking a chance on a new type of story.

To Amber, who is always a quick call or text away. I know you're tired of all my crazy ideas, but you always push me. Without you, I don't know how this story would have ever came to be. Thank you for (not) loving me.

To Dana, you are an inspiration and a reminder to always be my authentic self. Thank you for all the peen photos and the dirty talk... haha.

Ruth, you are my absolute favorite Canadian. Which is saying something considering my husband is also Canadian. I love the way you love and show up for those you care about. When I grow up, I want to be you.

My loving husband, thank you for the unlimited supply of water and food when I'm tied to the computer. Without you I would probably shrivel up and float away. I love you. Til the end.

To my annoyingly perfect children. Thank you for sharing me with the world and any characters that take up my time. Thank you for loving me.

And to you... the readers. Without you there wouldn't be a book. I am constantly amazed by your dedication and insastiable appetite for a good love story. I hope you enjoyed Weston and Lucy and remember to always get back up when life knocks you down.

about sutton snow

SUTTON SNOW IS a labor of love for me. and a dear friend. We have been weighing options for a while now, unsure if we should create a new pen name for the spicier books or publish everything under the our personal accounts.

In the end, we both decided to make something unique together.

If you are new here, and aren't aware, HI! My name is Tinley Blake. I will be writing under Sutton Snow along with a friend of mine (who is choosing to not be listed for now) for all our darker, spicier novels. I hope you have a look around and find something you like.

Visit her website to find out more:
Suttonsnow.com

Join her Facebook reader group:
Smutty Suttys
To contact Sutton, please email her at
author@suttonsnow.com

about
tinley blake

TINLEY BLAKE HAS SLEPT under the stars in Las Vegas, eaten dinner at midnight with French men who couldn't be trusted to keep their mouths on their food, and traveled across the countryside in stolen vehicles with worldwide drug men and lived to tell the tale.

She likes stories about family, loyalty, and extraordinary characters who struggle with basic human emotions while dealing with bigger than life problems. Tinley loves creating heroes who make you swoon, heroines who make you jealous, and the perfect Happily Ever After endings.

These days, you can find her writing in a sweet bungalow on the outskirts of Birmingham, Alabama, with her very own French man who is now her loving husband, their four kids, two dogs, and one very confused cat named Goat.

Visit her website to find out more:
Tinleyblake.com
Join her Facebook reader group:
Tinley Blake's Readers
To contact Tinley, please email her at
author@tinleyblake.com

author works

SECOND CHANCE ROMANCE
THE WAY WE LOVED
THE WAY WE FOUGHT

ENEMIES TO LOVERS
LIAR LIAR: VOLUME ONE

ROMANTIC COMEDY
SEXPLORATION
PARKER & ELIAS STORY

SPICY BOOKS
UNBROKEN
PACEY'S STORY

Printed in Great Britain
by Amazon

28498844R10121